FIRST MAITZ

MAITZ

SELECTED WORKS BY DON MAITZ

URSUS IMPRINTS • 5539 JACKSON • KANSAS CITY , MO • 64130

Library of Congress Catalog Number: 88-50651
ISBN 0-942681-01-0 Trade Edition
ISBN 0-942681-02-9 Signed/Slipcased/Limited Edition

Certain paintings reproduced in this book are available
as color lithographs, photoprints, or black and white prints.
For a current price list or additional information
send a self-addressed, stamped envelope to:
PAPER MAITZ, c/o Mr. & Mrs. Karl Maitz, 85 Ivy Road, Plainville, CT 06062

Printed and bound in the United States of America
First Edition
10 9 8 7 6 5 4 3 2 1

To my parents
Gladys and Karl Maitz

IN APPRECIATION

Many people have encouraged, inspired, and supported me throughout my career. To give them their due, they helped make this collection of works possible. The following individuals have worked directly on this book, and I would like to express my appreciation for their assistance and kind words:

Janny Wurts, Jonathan Matson, Natalie Schofield, Michael Whelan, Audrey Price, Pat Cadigan, Ray Fiest, Kathlyn Starbuck , and Irving Blomstrann.

The contributors, who have lent their views and their comments: James C. Christensen, Ken Davies, Rowland Elzea, Beth Fleisher, Gene Mydlowski, Amy Rowland, Keith Taylor, Ron Walotsky, and Gene Wolfe.

And my publishers, not the least of which are Arnie Fenner and Jim Loehr of Ursus Imprints.

Introduction

GENE WOLFE

There are many definitions of excellence in art, and many are mutually exclusive; possibly no single definition will satisfy even a simple majority of us. Excellent *cover* art, however, can be defined quite simply: it is art that is in the strict sense attractive. The real function of every piece of cover art is to facilitate the sale of the book or magazine it decorates. Most books and magazines are sold on the spot, and so it is necessary that a potential buyer notice this particular item in a display of hundreds or even thousands of similar items.

Furthermore, it is highly desirable that the item be picked up. Watch the browsers in a bookstore sometime, and you'll see that they look over hundreds of books they do not buy; but every fourth or fifth book that is actually handled is sold.

Don Maitz is a great cover artist because he creates images that attract your attention *and* make you want to study them more closely. As any publisher or art director will tell you, it is not an easy job. No doubt Don himself could tell you far better than I how he does it—but unlike Don (who's overmodest) and the publisher and art director (who would tell you they're too busy), I'm going to try. It seems to me that Don's pictures have at least three qualities that few other artists can match.

The first, of course, is sheer beauty. Have a look at the cover for Chelsea Quinn Yarbro's *Ariosto*, the one that made the rest of us want to choke her. The key element (barely glimpsed) is the sun, rising beyond the balustrade. We see the hero and the hippogriff, the pensive maiden and the terrace on which she stands, lit from behind and rendered with a pallet that is both dusky and radiant. The maiden, who seems to be about fourteen, is pretty at best. Lodovico looks stern and a trifle cruel; the hippogriff is less lovely than monstrous. Yet the composition as a whole is breathtaking: an unforgetable moment that has not yet been, never seen and recalled always.

The next is illustration, by which I mean the assurance we receive that the things pictured are in fact to be found within. No better example could be found than Maitz's magnificent pirate captain. This picture was not created for a book at all, but as an ad for rum. Henry Morgan's left foot is planted solidly upon the cask, and the ship that carried it is in the background. We see at once that there is treasure here, just as we know there is treasure of another kind in the tower of the sad wizard who sends forth Lodovico.

The last I would call *wit*, if I were not afraid you might misunderstand. Let us call it intelligence instead—a fiddling word, but the best we have now that wit has been reduced to gags and guffaws. Just look at Don's painting for *The Shadow of the Torturer*, one of the finest covers that I (or any other writer) have ever had. If you've read the book, you will grasp at once how perfectly this image captures its mood: the torturer masked, living, and silent; the skulls long-dead, yet snared in agony. We writers are prone to complain that the artists do not read our texts; but the fact is that it doesn't really matter whether they read them or not. What does matter enormously is whether they comprehend them. Don Maitz does, and in that comprehension stands virtually alone.

GENE WOLFE
Barrington, IL

Biography

SOLOMON KANE

BALANCE OF POWER

When asked about the start of his art career, in his honest moments, Don Maitz admits that he began with cave painting; out of respect for his mother, his early works are unavailable to the public. From there, he progressed to drawings on paper, any subject, any time there was a pencil and enough light. Although a better than average student—he received only two C's throughout high school—his goal was a career in art.

Solid, sensible people tried to advise him to aspire toward something more practical than struggling to enter a competitive and difficult field—but Don had other ideas. He attended night classes in figure drawing, then entered the Paier College of Art in Hamden, Connecticut, and immediately earned the envy of his peers. At Paier, under the influence of a distinguished roster of instructors, he began to paint, and by the time he graduated at the top of his class in 1975 he had already had work published by a professional magazine and in Marvel Comics. He stayed on for a fifth year at Paier and began to show his portfolio in New York.

Popularity put a stop to extra education as Don received his first paperback cover assignments. The works included in his first portfolio have been reproduced in the margins of these pages. The fact that Don's penchant for lousy puns didn't get him thrown out on the sidewalk forever is a testament to the strength of his abilities.

Bad puns notwithstanding, his reputation has only increased in stature, after some 150 paperback covers—one of which, "The Second Drowning," painted for a book entitled *The Road to Corlay*, won a silver medal at the Society of Illustrator's annual exhibition in 1980. That same year Don received the Howard Award for Best Artist at the World Fantasy Convention.

In addition to working for virtually all of the major paperback publishers in New York, Don's magic with the paintbrush produced the pirate image which launched Captain Morgan Spiced Rum to success in a marketplace where new products fail more often than not. Now Don's competitive colleagues can't even seek escape in the bars. The labels on the rum have his signature on them, as do billboards, T shirts, and beach towels.

Not being content with having science fiction and fantasy illustrations confined to the bookstores, Don was the driving force behind the first major museum exhibition of works within the field. Held at the New Britain Museum of American Art in spring of 1980, the show broke all previous attendence figures; that record holds today. Other museums have since launched similar exhibits, always with Maitz artwork included and always with public enthusiasm. Perhaps the most exciting of these was sponsored by NASA in conjunction with its 25th Anniversary celebration. Housed in the Cleveland Museum of Natural History, paintings by thirty science fiction artists were shown alongside photographs from the Apollo space program.

More recently, Don had four paintings in the first exhibition from the National Academy of Fantastic Art, held at the Delaware Museum. The paintings by Maitz were awarded the bronze medal (and not even that could stop the puns).

This success story might lead one to believe that Don Maitz is permanently attached to his paintbrush and inseparably chained to his easel. But between ideas, inspiration, and the deadlines that are inescapable in the illustration field, Don goes windsurfing, downhill skiing, waterskiing, and jogging. He also hangs out behind his camera lens—and in museums—continually adding to his stock of ideas.

He has shown himself willing to share his techniques, his enthusiasm, and his inventive imagination, by serving a year as guest instructor at the Ringling School of Art and Design in Sarasota, Florida. The impression he left on his students and fellow instructors has been permanent—and and it is hoped it will continue with the circulation of this book.

Of his beginnings, Don says, "In becoming a visual artist, I found myself faced with dilemmas. What subjects to realize—portraits, landscapes, still lifes, or abstracts? In what form should the subjects be represented—drawings, paintings, sculpture, or collage? How should I approach the subject—through impressionism, realism, surrealism, or abstract? Through experimentation, I found I enjoyed all of the above and could not make a choice as to which particular art form to claim as my own. I decided to enter a field where all of the above would be subject to my discretion. I attempted to show with conviction the furthest reaches of my imagination with whatever materials are suited to the occasion. By the process of observation, practice, and experimentation, my technique continually evolves. I have rendered in egg tempera, watercolor, graphite, pen and ink, pastel, charcoal, gouache, casein, alkyd, acrylic, and oil paint. I've experimented with a variety of applications: cross hatch, wet into wet, dry brush, splatter, scumbling, glazing, airbrush, dripping—and I've used everything from sponges, sand, salt, plastic wrap, palette knives, razor blades, sand paper, Q tips, and fingers to lay down paint on all kinds of surfaces. Canvas and masonite (Maitz-onite) are my favorite supports. The experience of creation is often an enjoyable one, and if my enjoyment is communicated to the viewer then I feel the artwork is a success.

"Calling myself a fantasy illustrator, by definition means that I am explaining, or exemplifying, imagination unrestrained by reality. My goal is to entertain visually, to produce a fantastic scene where make-believe, pretend, and 'what-if' run free. Illustrating book jackets calls for reflecting the nature of the author's ideas in a visually refreshing manner so that someone looking for diversion in the day-to-day routine will have, at a glance, some idea of the book's content and be entertained by the painting at the same time."

STAKEOUT   LITHOGRAPH PRINT

RUN AWAY, YOU FOOL

MAGIC POOL

LADY & HER PET   LIMITED EDITION LITHOGRAPH

Techniques
DON MAITZ

When I was just a twinkle in my parents' eye, waiting around the gene pool, this old guy in wild clothing came up to me and said, "Hey, wanna see what I can do?"

Being curious, and not yet evolved enough to have been warned about strangers, I said sure.

Well, the fellow pulls out these wild paintings—real eye-poppers. I asked, "Where do you get your ideas, how long does it take you to do one of these, where did you learn to do this, and most importantly, can you show me?"

He said he could teach me, but, as I was in a pre-fetal state of existance, I would have to wait a bit before I could practice the techniques. That's how I acquired my earliest art lessons—I guess you could call them the conceptual method of developing talent.

In response to the unanswered questions that a renowned colleague of mine raises elsewhere in this book, I have illustrated the wizard's methods, and provided text to explain how I have adapted his secrets into procedures I use to make paintings.

Step 1: THE SKETCH

Either a publisher sends me a manuscript to illustrate, or I have some concept to visualize that inspires me to pick up my sketchbook.

Several hasty scribbles are set down to test a variety of approaches. These may be tiny thumbnails, isolated details, or relatively small, detailed drawings. At this point, I do some inspirational research, enhancing my visualizations, or perfecting some technical detail I may be required to include. The best ideas are selected and then refined into color roughs used in preparation for the final painting.

Steps 2 & 3:
THE DRAWING
AND THE RESEARCH

Now I enlarge the most suitable of my sketches to the desired size, and set about making the image more accurate through a simultaneous combination of applied drawing, photography of models and props, and delving further into books and picture files. This process involves many overlays of tracing paper and a successive series of pencil images until I am satisfied.

Sometimes the changes and adjustments made to my original idea are extensive. If working under contract, I may send a copy of the drawing to the art director for further approval, to be certain such alterations will work and to provide final placement of my composition and enable the designer to place the type.

Step 4:
PREPARING THE SUPPORT

My most common choice of surface is untempered, gessoed masonite, textured or lightly sanded, depending on how I want the paint to go down. I have also used canvas, illustration board and wood panels. The subject matter of the painting always determines how I prepare the ground for the paint. The drawing is put onto the surface using a hard pencil and a graphite transfer sheet. At this stage, I usually refine the details one last time.

Step 5: THE UNDERPAINTING

From here, my technique tends to fly off on tangents, based entirely on what I see, what I have remembered, and those ideas I am trying to communicate. Depending on the image, I might be influenced by the work of other artists, places I have visited, and pictures in files and books. Generally, I begin with a tone washed thinly over the masonite—some areas may be masked off and left light, or glazed over with another color. Sometimes I paint over a simple base tone, the color of which would be determined by the overall mood I wish to achieve.

Step 6: THE BLOCK IN

Here, I lay in the basic colors of the piece and finalize the tonal effect, leaving details and subtleties loose.

Step 7: THE PAINTING

I have no set preference between oil or acrylic—based on years of experience and trial and error, I have developed my own foolproof method. I goop the paint out, wiggle things into it (usually paint brushes, but nothing in the house is really safe). Then I smear, puddle, and mix, until the Federal Express man comes and takes the painting out of my hands and delivers it to the publisher.

In every painting I do, I invent certain elements which come from my imagination. These may take the form of landscapes, costumes, props, creatures, or figures. Wherever possible, I prefer to substantiate my ideas, making the improbable situations I paint as realistic as I can through the use of photography and models. Friends and relatives are frequently drafted for this purpose.

The models used for this painting were brothers that went to grammar school with me. They enjoyed this opportunity to come to grips with their ongoing sibling rivalry. In the included photo you see how I took unfair advantage of my Dad's good nature. I had him put on kiddie goggles, strap a jigsaw puzzle box to his back, and asked him to grip a vacuum cleaner hose in his mouth while he climbed over our picnic table.

Naturally, with this sort of charade taking place in the back yard, the neighbors take notice. One became curious enough to stroll over for a closer look and, as one thing led to another, he ended up on the book cover, too.

Fortunately, my Dad has forgiven me for making a monkey out of him on my first commissioned book cover.

OIL ON CANVAS • 22 in. X 28 in.
VIRGIN AND THE WHEELS
BY L. SPRAGUE DE CAMP
POPULAR LIBRARY

ORIGINAL PAINTING IN THE COLLECTION OF ISAAC BEREZDIVIN

GALLERY

Don Maitz and I began our careers in this field in the same issues of Marvel sword and sorcery comics. That his work showed imagination and skill was obvious, especially to another newcomer eager to succeed in the cutthroat world of commercial illustration.

Later, I began to see his art on paperback covers, but it wasn't until we met at the World Fantasy Convention in Fort Worth that my curiosity was first aroused. He was busy pulling his paintings from a huge black box to hang them in the art show, so we shared a hasty handshake over it. I was busy, too, but I noticed something—he carefully closed the lid just before I approached him. Also, no illustrator I'd ever met was organized enough to have such a safe and secure way to transport his work and I was immediately struck by this inconsistency.

Later, Audrey and I attended a Halloween party at Don's house in Plainville. Throughout the entertaining though uneventful evening, that peculiar black box loomed in the corner. We left in the early hours of the morning and, once on I-84, I felt relieved somehow to be out of its presence. I was going to ask Audrey if she shared my curiosity about the black box, but didn't get the chance. We hit a twisted hunk of metal which caught on the transmission and forced us off the road. We were near one of Connecticut's highway amenities, the motorist call box, so I walked back to call a tow truck. I was sure I heard laughter in the bushes, but after all, this was Halloween.

I worked on the front end with the service man and the repairs held the rest of the way home. However, having narrowly escaped death, my concentration was so completely on getting us there safely that I forgot about the laughter, and I forgot to ask Audrey about the black box.

The following year Don's work appeared on covers for almost every major SF publisher. He also began working with curator F. Jacque von Schneden on putting together a group show of SF and fantasy art at the New Britain Museum of American Art. Once again my suspicions were aroused. In a world of self-seekers who often paint only for the dollar, Don has done much to advance interest in and appreciation for all SF and fantasy art. The success of the New Britain show was a boon for all of us and we have Don to thank for it, but this was decidedly unusual. It was almost as if he were creating a diversion—but from what, I wondered.

The Black Box. In the flourish of Don's success I'd forgotten about it, but as time

passed I became sure it held the key to the mystery. At a recent Boskone I finally had the opportunity to get near it again. First I saw it during the art show set-up as Don and I exchanged hellos and room numbers. But it wasn't until Saturday night that the time was right for a close examination. During the showing of the original "Nosferatu" with live organ accompaniment, those of us in the reserved section were enjoying a few beers provided by the Boskone staff. Audrey sat between Don and me and plied him with ale while I slipped out, got a key from the front desk (under some vague pretext) and dashed up to his room.

There I confirmed my wildest fears. Floating above the box was The Wiz-

ard—you know, that old gent Don has immortalized so well. There he was with his hookah and wine glass, exactly as pictured, but Don had omitted a few things: brushes, paint, and canvas! He heard my gasp and let go some Maitzean lightning as he sprung toward me. Eldritch lights flared, throwing shadows like a gigantic checkerboard over the walls. A grinning skull floated at me, cackling with menace. I reeled into the hall, with The Wizard in hot pursuit.

Now at a convention, a wizard doesn't attract much attention, so except for an occasional "Hey, nice costume!" he was free to give chase. He would've had me for sure then, save for my taking the stairs while he took the elevator. Everyone knows how long it takes a con elevator to get anywhere!

I made it back to the movie just in time to join the standing ovation for the organist. On seeing Don, The Wizard slunk out a side exit and I caught my breath. Now I was really confused. How was Don able to get The Wizard to do his painting for him? What hold on him did he have? And how could I get him to do the same for me? Did capturing his likeness also capture most of his powers?

Don's popularity and success continue to increase at an alarming rate, as does his health and good nature. If you have the pleasure of meeting him, you'll find him open and friendly and more than willing to chat about "his" work. Be sure to see "his" paintings at the various conventions and galleries, but use caution. Don has never mentioned my discovery and I am convinced that The Wizard cannot remain enslaved much longer. My friends, the next exhibit just may be the place where he plans to regain control and to claim his rightful place in the limelight as artiste, not model. Beware of the Black Box.

MICHAEL WHELAN
Hugo Award-winning Illustrator

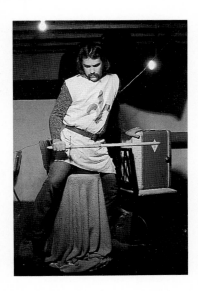

Upon graduation from art school, my first order of business was to refine the portfolio I was showing to publishers in New York. The Saint George and the Dragon theme became one of my subjects. When I showed this to an art director, by chance it happened that L. Sprague de Camp had written a story called "Two Yards of Dragon" which was to be published in an anthology. My painting, by coincidence, seemed to precisely illustrate a scene in the manuscript. So, with a few minor changes, this painting intended for my portfolio became the cover for a paperback book.

LITHOGRAPH PRINT

OIL ON WOOD PANEL • 29 in. X 19 in. • *FLASHING SWORDS #3* EDITED BY LIN CARTER • DELL PUBLISHING COMPANY

THE SECOND DROWNING

If any one particular painting of mine is a "landmark work," I suppose this would be it. At a time when science fiction covers were competing for attention with exaggerated action and color, this work stood out with its somber mood and limited palette. In 1980 the Society of Illustrators awarded it a silver medal in the book division—a rare feat for a fantasy painting. The National Book Council also gave it a nomination for one of the best overall paperback covers of that year.

Sometimes what I name a painting differs from the title of the published book, often because I wish to be inventive, or to emphasize some idea of my  own that is central to the work. However, I always read the author's story and derive as much inspiration as I can from it, maintaining the accuracy of the details.

The novel for which this painting was commissioned is about a great flood in the near future, much the same as the dunking associated with Noah. The cause of the cataclysm was surmised to be the result of the Lord's disapproval of our all-consuming dependence upon gadgets and our adulation of technology. The television antenna peeking above the surface of the water as the boat floats by symbolizes that technolgy has been "washed up" by divine intervention. The girl's companion was described as near death and I pictured her adrift, as if looking for something to believe in. Centered within the boat is the infamous Black Box mentioned earlier—the one my fellow artists in the field are all dying to look into. I thought that destruction and floods notwithstanding, some of my paintings would be preserved. I was hoping my hang-ups would still be around no matter what our future might hold.

LIMITED EDITION LITHOGRAPH

OIL ON MASONITE • 28 in. X 35 in.
THE ROAD TO CORLAY BY RICHARD COWPER
POCKET BOOKS

DISILLUSION/Pencil

A repeated theme in my work is to animate objects, giving inert things a life of their own. In this case the author wrote of an ominous fog sent by a wicked sorcerer to slay a princess. I invented nasty types to do the deed by placing plastic wrap in wet paint and imagining evil smoke-like critters suggested by the horrific shapes in the texture, much as if seeing faces or animals in clouds.

And speaking of clouds: while I was at my easel, a thunderstorm rolled past my studio window. I looked up to see if I needed to shut out any rain and instead reached for my paintbrush. I had to work in a flash to nail down the background that so conveniently happened by.

PHOTOPRINT

OIL ON MASONITE • 30 in. X 20 in. • *MONT CANT GOLD* BY PAUL R. FISHER • BERKLEY PUBLISHING GROUP

THE DUEL/Pen and Ink

This character wandered the world sending ghosts to their final rest. The seductive spectre lying in his path is trying to distract his attention while her henchmen come out of the scenery to do him in. In conversation with the author, she mentioned to me that the figure of the man, painted mostly from my imagination, looked just like the friend she had styled her character after. I suppose I chose the features as the spirit moved me.

LITHOGRAPH PRINT

OIL ON MASONITE • 30 in. X 20 in. • *KILL THE DEAD* BY TANITH LEE • DAW BOOKS

THE DAGGER /Pencil   BLACK AND WHITE PRINT

Intense. Energetic. Wild! Don Maitz's paintings are so powerful they claim center stage in any art show, and jump out at bookstore browsers from all over the stands.

He likes to tell the story of working on a painting in a basement studio one day, and turning around to discover a bunch of kids watching him intently through the window, captivated by the magical world he was making real with his paint brush. He goes about making the scene real by doing research. Like many artists, he keeps "morgue" files of clippings containing interesting photographs torn out of newspapers and magazines—anything that might lend itself to imaginative extrapolation required to make good fantasy and science fiction cover art. His own pho-

tographs of animals, landscapes, and architecture often go into this morgue file, too.

By using photographs of earthly creatures as basis for his alien monsters and domesticated beasts, Maitz is able to give the viewer the sense that these imagined creatures are anatomically accurate. Photographs only serve as visual references, however. Rather than copying them, Maitz works up four or five sketches—first in pencil, then in oil or acrylics—that arrange the elements of the scene he's chosen in several ways. Then he elaborates on these elements with imagination.

excerpted from an article
"Don Maitz and His
Magical Wand: A Paintbrush"
by Amy Zaffarano Rowland

LITHOGRAPH PRINT

OIL ON CANVAS • 24. in X 18 in. • *FLASHING SWORDS #4* EDITED BY LIN CARTER • DELL BOOKS

BIRD · OF · PARADISE

FLYING GOOSE/Pen and Ink

In a tale similar to Sinbad the Sailor, seven princesses don dresses of feathers and magically change into birds while the main character looks on in astonishment.

PHOTOPRINT

OIL ON MASONITE • 26 in. X 20 in. • *HASAN BY PIERS ANTHONY* • TOR BOOKS

RIDERS OF THE SIDHE • HESTIA • ARIOSTO

I was in the science fiction field for about 10 years before I started going to conventions. You never really meet other artists, but you know their work. You spend a lot of time in drugstores looking at paperback covers. I'd see Don's work all over the place; his style was out of the early days of illustration, by which I mean it had the feeling and look of the old master illustrators like Arthur Rackham or N.C. Wyeth.

I said to myself, "Hey, this guy can paint. He must have been painting for 20 or 30 years to get that good." Then I met Don for the first time at the 1980 Boston World Science Fiction Convention. What a shock! I was expecting some old guy and here was this young, good-looking, incredibly talented man. How depressing! Especially his original art work: paintings so beautiful they did not need a book or a story. They stood on their own as art. The texture of the work was wonderful; you cannot see that from reproductions.

I remember he was taking paintings out of his big Black Box, each new piece more amazing than the previous one. Here was this mild mannered man who looked like Clark Kent but who painted like Superman. Don seemed rather shy and didn't appear to listen to what I said. I thought he was a little spaced out. I've known a few other artists who were on their own trip through life, and who were all a little eccentric, but I found out later that it was

because I was standing on the wrong side of Don. He didn't hear what I was saying: he has a hearing problem in one ear and, naturally, I was talking to that one. So it turned out that he was not only a great painter, but a really good guy.

RON WALOTSKY
Illustrator

ALKYDS ON MASONITE • 30 in. X 20 in. • *RIDERS OF THE SIDHE* BY KENNETH C. FLINT • BANTAM BOOKS

OIL ON MASONITE • 24 in. X 20 in. • *HESTIA* BY C.J. CHERRYH • DAW BOOKS

OIL ON MASONITE • 27 in. X 32 in. • *ARIOSTO* BY CHELSEA QUINN YARBRO • POCKET BOOKS

Having the desire to become an artist (and having been captivated by books of adventure, science fiction and mythology during childhood), comic books satisfied my fascination with pictures and entertaining stories. Here were the heroes, monsters, villains and space ships that I enjoyed—but doing their thing in *pictures*. I drew my favorite characters again and again and eventually started to put them into a page format, redoing an existing comic story as if I had been the artist given the script. At the time I never realized what valuable groundwork I was establishing for my career.

When I entered art school I had already developed important creative skills from the comics I experimented with in my free time. I had already come to grips with the proportion, gesture and anatomy problems necessary to comic book art as well as drawing from life. The ability to exaggerate character and action focused my ability to understand, simplify and reposition a figure from my imagination at will. I did not realize that comic book drawings developed other skills needed to tell a story visually; freezing an action from a plot description, forming concepts into images and placing these in a composition under space restrictions; allowing for typography and arranging the images into a sequential format.

At art school I was exposed to new forms of representational art. For the first time I really saw the great paintings done throughout history, the original works of illustrators I had only known in reproductions. This exposure to new horizons made me want to experiment

THE CHECKERED CAPE/Pen and Ink

beyond the pencil/pen-and-ink media. I wished to create images a viewer could take in all at once rather than paging through a sequential format. The transition was difficult. At first I struggled to translate my experience with drawing in line to painting in tones, but the challenge did not overcome my enthusiasm. I applied myself to painting the model from life and gradually gained confidence. The cover illustration marketplace offered singular advantages: use of full color, return of my originals, a byline for doing the entire illustration—*and* I got to read the novels.

OIL ON MASONITE • 30 in. X 20 in. • *FANE* BY DAVID M. ALEXANDER • POCKET BOOKS

Many artists complete paintings from sketchy pencil roughs. I prefer to go on from this stage and work up my preliminary concepts in full color, just a little larger than the paperback itself. It's here that I solve any problems that might arise so that when I execute the finished painting I have a guideline in front of me that sets the mood and which gives the art director, the publisher and myself a perspective on the final illustration.

In this case I tried to create an incident that shows an intelligent species of plant-life in the act of trying to wrest domination of the world from the human race. Although this specific scene was never written in the novel, I focused on one individual—the princess—to dramatize the fate of her entire kingdom. Moss is causing the castle fortifications to crumble and the ivy has flung open the window to kidnap the girl. I mixed sand into the gesso under the stonework to lend realistic texture to the paint.

LITHOGRAPH PRINT

OIL ON MASONITE • 30 in. X 20 in. • *THE GREEN GODS* BY N.C. HENNEBERG TRANSLATED BY C.J. CHERRYH • DAW BOOKS

The conflict is (surprise!) good versus evil, symbolized by the forces of light and darkness doing battle through magic.

ACRYLIC ON MASONITE • 30 in. X 20 in. • *HAWKS OF FELLHEATH* BY PAUL R. FISHER • BERKLEY PUBLISHING GROUP

 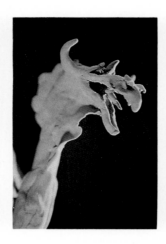 

The scene I chose to illustrate this book brought to mind the well-known sequence from the film *Jason and the Argonauts*, animated by Ray Harryhausen—except here we have a character whose sorcery causes the skeletons to come alive and slay a dragon. The accompanying photos show my approach to the research for the final painting, based upon preliminary sketches pictured from my imagination and helped along by ideas and images from my "morgue" file. The sketches went off to the art director who selected one for the cover. Then began the process of researching for the final.

The dragon, made specifically as I visualized it from the story, was sculpted in clay and photographed. From the picture file I selected appropriate textures which might look plausible as dragon skin. The local college allowed me to arrange and photograph the plastic skeleton in their science department, which involved hooking the arms to a bulletin board. Slides and books of weapons and armor were used to fill in the other elements depicted in the illustration.

OIL ON MASONITE • 30 in. X 20 in. • *CURSE OF SAGAMORE* BY KARA DALKEY • BERKLEY PUBLISHING GROUP

SEALLEVEL

Although I much prefer to read an author's entire manuscript, in this case I was supplied only with an excerpt, character descriptions and an outline.

Basically we have a love triangle. The tide is coming in, splashing around the harpist's ankles. Her fiance has followed her to the shore; he is about to get a surprise because his intended is a selkie, and will turn into a seal when she gets wet. The nudging seal (her boyfriend from the sea) has brought his family along to entice her. She is torn between her magical life and her husband-to-be on dry land.

A friend who is an accomplished harpist posed for the heroine.

OIL ON MASONITE • 26 in. X 35 in.
THE WORLD INVISIBLE
BY SHULAMITH OPPENHEIM
BERKLEY PUBLISHING GROUP

When commisioned to do a series the artist has the opportunity to do progressional statements. Here, the combined work is entitled *Book of the New Sun*. I began with a gray painting and, with each cover, manipulated my use of color to show the dawning of a new sun, a new consciousness, a new era, through increased color intensity.

The profession of cover illustrator can often be a hectic one. Many times, caught in conflict between deadlines and trying to achieve high artistic standards, a painter can come to feel as though his head is on the block. I like to hide my signature within the context of the painting: here I could not resist the inclination to chalk myself up neckst.

OIL ON MASONITE • 30 in. X 20 in. • *SWORD OF THE LICTOR* BY GENE WOLFE • POCKET BOOKS

OIL ON MASONITE • 30 in. X 20 in. • *CLAW OF THE CONCILIATOR* BY GENE WOLFE • POCKET BOOKS

OIL ON MASONITE • 30 in. X 20 in. • *CITADEL OF THE AUTARCH* BY GENE WOLFE • POCKET BOOKS

While on a quest, this heroine is sent by ungenerous townspeople to confront a dragon, but with inadequate equipment: a stick for a lance, an old, cast-off shield and a plow horse. The expression of her mount and the flies buzzing around its head pretty much set the mood for the piece. The dragon has a pretty good reason to be grouchy, since she herself is a princess under enchantment.

OIL ON MASONITE • 30 in. X 20 in. • *WITCHDAME* BY KATHLEEN SKY • BERKLEY PUBLISHING GROUP

Sketchbook pages for MIRROR OF HELEN

Painting is, by nature, a solitary process. Even if he spends time in the classroom or dealing with art directors or occasionally meeting the public at a gallery or convention, the painter eventually finds himself back in the studio, alone, and that is where the real work happens. Facing the canvas or board with a possibly great idea, a deadline looming just beyond the light, a heart full of hope and a head full of self doubt and insecurity, the artist is very alone. Cajoled by the promise of great accomplishment and confronted by the possibility of humiliating failure, the artist must battle his personal demons on a daily basis.

Few people can actually comprehend how tough it is to be a painter. I think only other artists can really empathize and we need occasional reassurance that we are not the only ones confronting these constant contradictions. That's why I'm writing this for Don. He's a kindred spirit and, from time to time, we take a break from "the struggle" to help each other out.

Whether I go to the East Coast on business, or lure Don out here to Utah to ski for a few days—even if it has been a year since we've seen each other, it only takes about eight seconds for us to re-establish a comfortable rapport and mutually uplifting (and largely zany) dialogue. I am fortunate to count Don as a friend. His work delights and inspires me. His wit cheers me up, and his willingness to share ideas and feelings makes it easier to go back to the studio with the comforting thought that at least one other crazy is out there who shares my excitement and insecurity. I hope that I do some of that for Don, too. We each need all the help we can get. Nobody's perfect, but Maitz makes imperfection at least tolerable, and at times, even enjoyable!

OK, Maitz, enough nice talk, now back to the drawing board. You've got work to do!!

JAMES C. CHRISTENSEN
Illustrator/Fine Artist/Assoc. Professor of Art
at Brigham Young University

ORIGINAL PAINTING IN THE COLLECTION OF RAYMOND E. FEIST

The heroine fell ill, the hero sprained his ankle, and left no other choice, the two had to entrust their fate to a disreputable-looking wizard whose spells work only on things that were once alive. Hence, the basket and the rope are enslaved to the wizard's will, since they are made from organic materials.

The tree, which is dying and almost subject to the wizard's domination, is grabbing the rope with its roots—and the rope, kicking up leaves in protest, is being scolded not to wake the girl.

The swollen ankle in the painting was my own, injured at the time while jogging, and the tree was inspired by a similar one I chanced upon in Central Park.

I was delighted by your cover painting for my novel, Bard.

I wondered a lot while the book was in preparation about the cover it would be published with. I knew a book's visual attractiveness has a lot to do with its sales, and I've seen many cover illos which had nothing to do with the contents. So while hoping for the best I prepared myself for disappointment.

Disappointed, I wasn't. Besides being striking, intriguing, and beautifully done, your painting shows an accurate scene from the story even to such details as Regan's black hair and the bard's swollen foot! The "face" on the dead oak with its split trunk was a lovely touch.

Thank you.

KEITH TAYLOR
Hawthorn, Australia

OIL ON MASONITE • 30 in. X 20 in. • *BARD* BY KEITH TAYLOR • BERKLEY PUBLISHING GROUP

OIL ON MASONITE • 30 in. X 20 in. • *BARD II* BY KEITH TAYLOR • BERKLEY PUBLISHING GROUP

OIL ON MASONITE • 30 in. X 20 in. • *BARD III: THE WILD SEA* BY KEITH TAYLOR • BERKLEY PUBLISHING GROUP

OIL ON MASONITE • 30 in. X 20 in. • *BARD IV: GATHERING OF RAVENS* BY KEITH TAYLOR • BERKLEY PUBLISHING GROUP

PUTTING OUT THE PRINCE/Pen and Ink

    This pen-and-ink explains how the frog prince got to the moat where he needs to entice a princess to kiss him and break his curse. I am sure he lost his looks in the first place because he got under-foot in the wizard's laboratory when the crotchety fellow was having a "bad spell."

    —In a green bottle.
    —In a green bottle...
    —In a green bottle in a country where I, my children, have never been, sat a greybeard wizard. The wizard had a red bottle but he was trapped in a greenbottle, greenbottle redbottle, no sun no wind no rain and never never never so much as to hear or see a bluebottle...
    —In a green bottle...

from *Wizard War* by Hugh Cook

ACRYLIC ON MASONITE • 30 in. X 20 in. • *WIZARD WAR* BY HUGH COOK • WARNER BOOKS

This character is trying to fend off more adversaries than he can possibly slay, and, unaware of the wizard whose spell is about to rescue him, he is wondering which dragon is going to leap at him first.

I have been told that an artist is only as good as his research. This is true, to a point; I believe the creativity the artist can assert in assembling an image while utilizing the information is of equal importance.

The right mood, character, and emotion should carry more emphasis than the unvarnished reality of model, props, and costume. I want to take liberties, make my inspiration and goals the driving force; otherwise I would only be copying and retaining all of the limitations inherent in the material in front of me. Any photo research I obtain simply becomes a departure point for my imagination.

Ongoing study of the figure and drawing from life adds to the working knowledge which allows me to drama-

tize gesture and expression for effect.

In 1985/86, I spent a year as a full-time visting instructor at the Ringling School of Art and Design in Sarasota, Florida. While teaching two entire days and three afternoons, I was also completing a book cover a month for various New York publishers. I became acquainted with a theatrical costume warehouse, the school library, photography department, and of course, many art students. These new resources were pooled together to help me with my assignments. Bard is one such painting. The pictured scene symbolizes the arrival of the Celts from northern Spain and their meeting with the ancient magical race already inhabiting Ireland.

OIL ON MASONITE • 30 in. X 20 in. • *BARD* BY MORGAN LLEWELYN • TOR BOOKS

Har! Ship Maitz rum! Since painting the label for this product, I always keep some on hand to ease the trials and tribulations of an illustrator's life. The following are some misadventures which give me reason to occasionally hit the bottle:

—original wet oil sketches due to be delivered the next day get run over by automobiles outside of a McDonald's on a slushy winter day;

—a painting stepped on by a printer who left behind a size 9D footprint and a large crack in quarter-inch-thick masonite;

—two stolen paintings, and a large one reputedly delivered strapped to the back of a bicycle messenger who pedaled through rain and New York traffic;

—a painting crunched by UPS, and several others misplaced and misrouted by airlines;

—a nearly completed wet oil original nibbled by a red squirrel.

OIL ON MASONITE • 38 in. X 28 in. • CAPTAIN MORGAN CO. BALTIMORE, MARYLAND

CAPTAIN MORGAN ORGINAL SPICED RUM / PUERTO RICAN RUM WITH SPICE AND OTHER NATURAL FLAVORS / 70 PROOF / CAPTAIN MORGAN RUM CO. / BALTIMORE, MD

TAPESTRY OF TIME

This is the sequel to "The Second Drowning." This time, the futuristic elements are represented by some decaying telephone poles with fallen wires in the distance. The stairway in the upper right corner represents the ascent into the hereafter.

OIL ON MASONITE • 23 in. X 31 in.
TAPESTRY OF TIME
BY RICHARD COWPER • POCKET BOOKS

I've seen a deal of war, and agree with Sherman that it's hell, but the Mutiny was the Seventh Circle under the Pit. Of course, it had its compensations: for one, I came through it, pretty whole, which is more than Havelock and Harry East and Johnny Nicholson did, enterprising lads that they were. (What's the use of a campaign if you don't survive it?) I did, and it brought me my greatest honour (totally undeserved, I needn't tell you), and a tidy enough slab of loot which bought and maintains my present place in Leicestershire—I reckon the plunder's better employed keeping me and my tenants in drink, than it was decorating a temple for the edification of a gang of blood-sucking priests. And along the Mutiny road I met and loved that gorgeous wicked witch Lakshmibai—there were others, too, naturally, but she was the prime piece.

from Flashman in the Great Game
by George MacDonald Fraser

ORIGINAL PAINTING IN THE COLLECTION OF DICK BRISSON

Production of a book always involves a whole team of professionals within the publishing business, primary among them the editor and the art director, whose expertise and guidance help both author and artist give the story and its cover their final form.

The Wicked Enchantment *is my favorite book from childhood. I must have read it twenty times. I was very excited to bring it out in paperback, and introduce the book to a whole new generation of kids. Don Maitz's painting captures what, for me, is the most tense and magical scene in the book: how the wicked housekeeper and her son are lured back to their niche in the facade of the old German cathedral, and are transformed back into a statue and a gargoyle, just as the clock strikes midnight. I can't think of anything that Don could have done differently to illustrate this scene better.*

BETH FLEISHER
Editor/Berkley Publishing Group

The Wicked Enchantment *is a perfect example of Don Maitz's abilities as an illustrator and also, just as important, his abilities as a communicator.*

It is a painting that would not be quickly identified as a "classic Maitz sf/fantasy cover." But to me, it is one of my favorites, and I think it exemplifies all of his strengths and traits as an illustrator.

It shows his strong sense of design; a simple, center-weighted image, symmetrical yet not mirror-like. The slight upward movement of the statues on the

right rescues it from being too static, and there is just enough visual information to "suggest" that there is something interesting and magical going on.

This painting is an excellent showcase for his drafting and painting skills. The rendering of the stone statues, the architectural details, and the foreshortening of the gargoyle at the top all act as

a perfectly cold, lifeless backdrop for the parrot; who, full of life, is caught in mid-flight, wings outstretched and virtually weightless, its strong talons delicately clutching the fragile mouse.

The painting also shows Don's knowledge of color. I've always thought of this as a perfect example of isolated, or limited, color. The statue, stone cold, is brought to life by the introduction of warm flesh tones and expressive gestures. The parrot, his feathers lush and multi-hued, is handled just right—down to the red in his legs (which brings your attention to the mouse.) Finally, the touch of red in the gargoyle's eyes serves two purposes. One—they give him life and the start of a personality, and two—they keep the viewer's eyes moving up and down the painting, a trick which enhances the composition.

All of these subtle elements add up to the fact that this is a successful illustration, well thought out, and masterfully executed.

This is where Don Maitz is a communicator. In a genre where the norm is to "illustrate a scene from the book," he usually goes beyond that. He has captured a moment in time, suggested mystery, wit, and magic, and, most of all, left enough to the imagination and expectation to make the potential reader want to buy the book and enter the world of fantasy that the cover art promises.

The Society of Illustrators also liked the painting enough to include it in their best of the year show.

GENE MYDLOWSKI
Senior Art Director
Berkley Publishing Group

The hero of this trilogy is a being from another dimension. Supernaturally bearlike and wolflike in its original form, it survives by recreating the body of a human host who has recently died. It begins as a child, a young boy who drowned, and in this guise is taken in by a farm couple. The creature retains the ability to shift form between beast and man. It grows to maturity, retaining influences and traits from each side of its dual nature, which sometimes cause conflicts. The illustration shows the shift from boy to other dimensional being.

OIL ON MASONITE • 23 in. X 20 in. • *THE ORPHAN* BY ROBERT STALLMAN • POCKET BOOKS

T H E · C A P T I V E

The sequel to *The Orphan* deals with the being in an older form, and in another human persona. He marries and acquires a stepdaughter. When the wife and little girl are captured by baddies, the beast comes to the rescue.

In the last book, he and his mate change form and depart to another dimension.

This series was painted with a minimum of reference material, but I relied heavily upon the author's descriptions.

The Beast, third cover in the Stallman series.

OIL ON MASONITE • 22 in. X 20 in. • *THE CAPTIVE* BY ROBERT STALLMAN • POCKET BOOKS

F A E R I E · T A L E

At the heart of Faerie Tale *lies the confrontation between the mundane and the fantastic. Don's cover illustration of my book, used on the signed and numbered limited edition and the British edition, realizes all those elements in that confrontation. At the center of the work lies the sleeping Patrick (the fairy stone around his neck courtesy of*

OIL ON MASONITE • 16 in. X 36 in. • *FAERIE TALE* BY RAYMOND E. FEIST • HILLHOUSE PUBLISHING CO. & GRAFTON BOOKS, UK

artistic license) over whom hovers the Bad Thing. All that is innocent and beautiful juxtaposed against that which is horrific, good menaced by evil, that instant before contact when the inevitability of terror is before us, yet not quite upon us. Behind them, we see the prosaic image of the Hastings' house outlines against the red sunset of the Western sky, and as night falls we are shown how thin is the boundary between the mortal world and the world of the fairies. Fantastic figures ride in the distance and we see in Don's art both that which we know and that which we fear to know. It is rare for an author to see something that so graphically captures the heart of his work, but in this painting, Don has distilled down the strongest images from the book. It is an outstanding illustration, and to have had even an indirect influence upon this painting is a source of personal pride.

RAYMOND E. FEIST
author of *Faerie Tale*

Often I am asked how long it takes to complete a painting. A precise answer is difficult to determine. How much easier my life would be if I could determine an exact time in advance! Quite often I must decide upon my schedule in the space of a telephone call, and most occasions I'll have only the vaguest notion of the subject matter I am called upon to illustrate. Even the manuscript is an unknown factor: some read easily, some are long or slow or don't fit well into visual terms. I might be starting out exhausted from the last assignment, or be set back by unscheduled corrections. The sketches vary from job to job. Sometimes they happen quickly. Pictures just form in my mind and they look just as good on paper as they do in my imagination.

Other times, I am unsure of my images, and eight, nine, or ten drawings will be completed, with me still scribbling when the art director asks for something in the mail. On an average, a detailed color sketch takes approximately a full day to complete.

It is probably self-evident that the more figures and elements proposed in the sketch, the more I must involve myself with research; too much of this can stifle the fun and imagination which give the image that indefinable spark of life I strive to achieve.

Sometimes the opposite happens. After being exposed to the all pervasive graffiti during my visits to New York, I decided the Borrible characters in this book would be fellow perpetrators, in the backstreets of Lon-

don where they live. I tried to bring some of their sense of mischief and humor to their drab alley environment.

Inspiration of this sort tends not to work on a timetable. Many times, I have to step away from a work, give my mind a rest from the subject in order to see what I have, and then add the final touches that make the work truly finished. Deadlines can interfere with this process, and when a painting comes back from production, I know at a glance what needs to be done. The work goes back on the easel before framing, and, if this interval is a necessary part of the process also, then how long does it take me to complete a painting? Only the wizard knows for sure. He always works on Maitz-a-night.

ACRYLIC ON MASONITE • 30 in. X 20 in. • *THE BORRIBLES GO FOR BROKE* BY MICHAEL DE LARRABEITI • BERKLEY PUBLISHING GROUP

Asked to illustrate a collection of short stories which were set in India's future, I chose to focus upon a cultural tradition of relating tales through the symbolism and gestures of their ritualized dance. The past civilization had been devastated by war and lay in ruins; the new society built modern cities over the rubble. To imply this phoenix-like transformation, the omnipotent paintbrush became a poly-neutron-disintegration weapon, blasting out the ancient temple and blameless tree, setting the stage for the dancer's narrative.

OIL ON MASONITE • 30 in. X 20 in. • *TAMASTARA* BY TANITH LEE • DAW BOOKS

In my opinion, a successful painting must fulfill several requirements. It has to be attractive, both from a distance, and upon closer examination. It should raise questions with the viewer, and leave the impression of things about to happen; and enough information should be present to lend personality to the characters, while giving some indication of their quest, predicament, or whatever element may be involved.

The final painting reproduced on the paperback book cover is a small format to showcase all these points— particularly with the inclusion of typography, and the distraction of a hundred other releases which typically crowd the book stands. Dramatic steps must sometimes be taken with the composition to grab the browser's attention. If, at a glance, the viewer can be intrigued enough to ask, "What's going on here?" he will be more likely to pick up the book for a closer look.

In the accompanying work, the dramatic lighting on the character of the girl lends a sense of mystery and magic through a geometric shape that spotlights the moment when a spell is energized.

OIL ON MASONITE • 30 in. X 20 in. • *THE KEEPER'S PRICE* BY MARION ZIMMER BRADLEY • DAW BOOKS

The ship in this painting could move through time as well as space. I tried to depict the difficult concept of a ship that remained stationary, while, with the passage of time, the universe expanded around it. On this journey, the ship crossed a boundary into a region inhabited by ghosts, and her crew members are haunted as a result. This was one of my first opportunities to experiment with a new toy, the airbrush I purchased during my time as an instructor in Florida. Being in a position where I had to critique students who did airbrush work in their assignments, I was driven to learn something of the technique so that I could offer guidance fairly. In the process, I picked up some useful knowledge that contributed to my own paintings.

ACRYLIC ON MASONITE • 26 in. X 20 in. • *GHOST* BY PIERS ANTHONY • TOR BOOKS

While attending a museum reception which featured an exhibit that included a few of my paintings, I was approached by an elderly gentleman. Looking distinguished in a three-piece suit, he was staring intently at one of my illustrations. He politely inquired if I was the artist. I said that yes, I was. He looked back at the painting, then turned quizzically to me and asked in all seriousness, "What do you eat?"

For once I was at a loss for words. Using hindsight, I should have replied that I have a most colorful palate.

ORIGINAL PAINTING IN THE COLLECTION OF ELIZABETH R. WOLLHEIM

In a future society, ugliness became eliminated through genetic manipulation. One accidental, illegitimate child was born homely and deformed. At the urging of an avantgarde scientist of somewhat questionable motives, she became the basis of his research. While her body lived encased in a capsule, her conciousness was transferred into the body of the most beautiful android. The story focused on her struggle to cope with the change. Where once she was stared at with loathing, now she is relentlessly admired.

The painting began with the transfer of the drawing onto a middle-value blue tone. I puddled acrylic paint in the region of the figure's hair and blew it with a straw to make the wild, jagged patterns that imply the woman's confusion, as well as refer to the title of the novel.

PHOTOPRINT

ACRYLIC ON MASONITE • 30 in. X 20 in. • *ELECTRIC FOREST* BY TANITH LEE • DAW BOOKS

BORN
FOR THE FUTURE

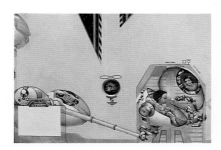

From the word "freezer" through the progression of symbols, and tanks with developing embryos which proceed right to left, I am trying to illustrate cloning, and the concept of mechanized, controlled birth. The cold grays and whites lend a sense of sterility to the environment, and the hazard symbols alongside the windows signify the poisonous atmosphere of a colonized, alien planet. Not only did this book involve recreating the organic structure, it explored the idea of regenerating the personality and abilitiesof the parent intact. The baby in the mechanical cradle is the clone of the powerful politician and scientist behind the research project in which her double is created. The predecessor, on screen, was modeled after the author. She is giving warning to her clone, both visually and via the connecting wire, that enemies will once again seek her life, and try to thwart her ambitions.

While reading the manuscript, I had a powerful image of a locket, or sense of tradition, handed down from mother to daughter, and of an egg, to symbolize birth. These shapes were combined in the baby's cradle. The rectangular white area in the lower left corner is for the UPC symbol. I wanted this to become a part of the illustration, as if each child has its own code classification to provide identification for the technicians.

ACRYLIC & OIL ON MASONITE
22 in. X 32 in.
CYTEEN BY C.J. CHERRYH • WARNER BOOKS

FREEZER

This character is trapped in a void between heaven and hell, surrounded by lost souls. The accompanying black-and-white shows a finished painting which was approved at sketch stage by the art director, but turned out too much like a horror cover to suit the novel it was intended for. The editors turned it down, asking for a solution that reflected a more science fiction approach. The grim reaper this time appears as a constellation opposite the figure of the man.

ACRYLIC ON MASONITE • 30 in. X 20 in. • *PURGATORY ZONE* BY ARSEN DARNAY • BERKLEY PUBLISHING GROUP

W A V E · W I T H O U T · A · S H O R E

ALFA/Pen and Ink

The artist described in this story was reputed to be the most talented wonder in the universe. Of course, I knew the perfect model for the job: me. The indigenous life-form of the colonized planet is acting the part of bystander, representing the cultural exchange which might result from space travel.

The background was done before I owned an airbrush. The even tone was produced by careful layering of wet acrylic glazes.

ACRYLIC ON MASONITE • 30 in. X 20 in. • *WAVE WITHOUT A SHORE* BY C.J. CHERRYH • DAW BOOKS

INTERIOR DESIGN:
JIM LOEHR & ARNIE FENNER

JACKET DESIGN AND HANDLETTERING:
ARNIE FENNER

The text of this book was digitally set in
Goudy Old Style, Bodoni, and Futura Book by Type, Inc.